Magic Marcus

by Elizabeth Dale and Gareth Conway

FRANKLIN WATTS

LONDON•SYDNEY

Chapter 1

Marcus was so excited as he rushed to
the toy stall at the school fete. Last year he'd
found a brilliant robot, even though it had only
worked for a while. This time he hoped to spend
his pocket money on another wonderful toy.
But nothing caught his eye ... until he looked
more closely.

Marcus pulled a stick out from under the toys.

It was made of wood and had strange symbols

carved along the side. A shiver went down his spine.

Could it possibly be a magic wand? He held it up.

"How much is this?" he asked the lady at the stall.

"Oh, that's not for sale," she said.

"Oh," Marcus frowned. "Why not? Is it yours?"

"No!" the lady laughed. "It's just an old stick!"

An old stick? Marcus stared at her. Hadn't she seen

the marks on it? It must be more than a stick, surely?

"It was put in with the toys by mistake," the lady said.

"Please put it in the bin for me."

Marcus eagerly took the wand away before the lady changed her mind. He wasn't going to throw it away — he'd got a wand that might just be magic! He tingled with excitement.

He knew just what he would do with it.

Marcus hurried over to his mum on the tea stall.

"I want to go home to check Benjy is all right,"

he said. "Is that okay, Mum?"

"Yes, as long as Becky goes with you," smiled

his mum.

Chapter 2

As Marcus went home with his sister, Becky, he worried about Benjy. Their dog had been sick and off his food for days. Marcus looked at his wand again. He really hoped it wasn't just a stick with strange carvings. He was sure it was magic!

When Becky opened the back door, Marcus
was greeted by an excited Benjy. Marcus knelt
down to cuddle him. Benjy licked Marcus's face.
"Hello, Benjy. How are you, boy?" Marcus said.
"Don't worry. Benjy looks better now,"
said Becky.

Becky went up to her room to listen to music.

Now, it was time for Marcus to use his magic.

He waved his wand and said:

"Magic wand – make Benjy better!"

And then he said, "Go, boy! Go and eat!"

Straight away, Benjy padded into the kitchen,

and up to his food bowl.

Marcus followed him excitedly. Benjy was eating again. Surely Benjy hadn't got better on his own? The magic had worked!

Chapter 3

Marcus laughed. "I'm magic!" he told Benjy.

Benjy woofed happily and ate more dinner.

"What shall I do next?" Marcus wondered,

walking into the lounge. Then, he had an idea.

Nobody could ever find the remote control
in their house. Sure enough, it was nowhere
to be seen. So he waved his magic wand again.
"Magic wand, make the remote control appear!"
he cried.

Suddenly, Marcus saw the remote. It was there on the floor. He could see it clearly. He laughed. He was sure it hadn't been there before.

"You see," Marcus cried, picking it up, "magic!"

Benjy woofed, excitedly.

"I'll do something more difficult now," said Marcus. He ran upstairs but was careful not to disturb Becky.

Marcus brought down his broken robot from last
year's school fete. Maybe his magic wand would
make it work now?
He stood it on the floor and then set up
an obstacle course with cushions.
"Robot, use your powers to find me!" he cried.
But nothing happened.

Marcus frowned. Then he realised he'd forgotten to wave his wand. So he waved it, saying "Robot, use your powers to find me!" Still nothing happened.

Marcus was upset.

He really wanted his robot to work again.

"Robot move!" he cried, waving his wand, madly.

CRASH!

Marcus gasped with horror. Waving his wand had somehow knocked his mum's favourite vase off the shelf. It was smashed to pieces!

Marcus felt terrible. And now Becky would be cross with him. Marcus waited, but Becky didn't come downstairs. "Maybe she is listening to music and didn't hear anything," he thought.

Chapter 4

Suddenly, Marcus saw his mum walking down

the path. He had to tidy up before she got inside!

"Magic wand, mend the vase and tidy up!"

he cried, waving it desperately.

But nothing happened.

His mum was opening the back door.

She'd be inside any minute. She'd see all the mess!

Marcus waved his wand again.

"Magic wand, stop Mum being cross with me!"

he cried.

Marcus's mum walked into the lounge

and stared at the mess everywhere.

As Marcus hurriedly picked up cushions and flowers,

Benjy ran round, yapping and jumping up wildly.

He was knocking off cushions as quickly as Marcus

replaced them!

"I'm really sorry, Mum," said Marcus.

His mum looked shocked, but she smiled at Marcus.

"Thank you for tidying up," she said.

Marcus gasped. She wasn't cross. His magic had worked! He was delighted.

Chapter 5

Then Mum's voice changed.

"I can tell you're better. You're being naughty again!" she said to Benjy. "Go into the kitchen!"

Marcus frowned. His mum thought that Benjy had made all the mess, not him.

"Bad, bad dog!" she cried.

Benjy padded sadly into the kitchen.

Marcus felt terrible. Benjy was in trouble
and it was all his fault.

"It wasn't Benjy. It was me!" Marcus said,

as his mum started tidying up the broken vase.

"I knocked the vase over, Mum!"

His mum turned and looked at him.

"I didn't mean to," said Marcus. "I know

it was your favourite vase. I'm really sorry."

Marcus's mum hugged Marcus.

"Thank you," she said. "Accidents can happen,

but what's important is that you told me the truth.

I'm proud of you. I'll always love you,

whatever you do."

Becky opened the door and Benjy came running in, happily. Marcus smiled. Not only had he made Benjy better, but he'd owned up and his mum wasn't angry. What a truly magical day!

Things to think about

1. Why does Marcus keep the stick?
2. How does Marcus try to show the stick is magic?
3. What does his Mum do when she finds her broken vase? Who does she think is to blame?
4. Why does Marcus own up to the accident in the end?
5. What lessons do you think Marcus has learnt?

Write it yourself

One of the themes in this story is telling the truth. Now try to write your own story about a similar theme.

Plan your story before you begin to write it.
Start off with a story map:
• a beginning to introduce the characters and where your story is set (the setting);
• a problem which the main characters will need to fix in the story;
• an ending where the problems are resolved.

Get writing! Try to use interesting phrases such as "he tingled with excitement" to describe your story world and excite your reader.

Notes for parents and carers

Independent reading

This series is designed to provide an opportunity for your child to read independently, for pleasure and enjoyment. These notes are written for you to help your child make the most of this book.

About the book

Marcus is looking for something special to buy at his school fete. Nothing catches his eye, until he spots a very strange-looking wooden stick. Could it possibly be a magic wand?

Before reading

Ask your child why they have selected this book. Look at the title and blurb together. What do they think it will be about? Do they think they will like it?

During reading

Encourage your child to read independently. If they get stuck on a word, remind them that they can sound it out in syllable chunks. They can also read on in the sentence and think about what would make sense.

After reading

Support comprehension and help your child think about the messages in the book that go beyond the story, using the questions on the page opposite.

Give your child a chance to respond to the story, asking:

Did you enjoy the story and why?

Who was your favourite character?

What was your favourite part?

What did you expect to happen at the end?

Franklin Watts
First published in Great Britain in 2018
by The Watts Publishing Group

Series Editors: Jackie Hamley and Melanie Palmer
Series Advisors: Dr Sue Bodman and Glen Franklin
Series Designer: Peter Scoulding

A CIP catalogue record for this book is
available from the British Library.

ISBN 978 1 4451 6304 8 (hbk)
ISBN 978 1 4451 6306 2 (pbk)
ISBN 978 1 4451 6305 5 (library ebook)

Printed in China

Franklin Watts
An imprint of
Hachette Children's Group
Part of The Watts Publishing Group
Carmelite House
50 Victoria Embankment
London EC4Y 0DZ

An Hachette UK Company
www.hachette.co.uk

www.franklinwatts.co.uk